Dad Goes to School

by Michèle Dufresne

PIONEER VALLEY EDUCATIONAL PRESS, INC.

Dad is in the office.

Dad is in the cafeteria.

Dad is in the art room.

Dad is in the computer room.

Dad is in the library.

11

Dad is in the gym.

13

Dad is in the nurse's office.

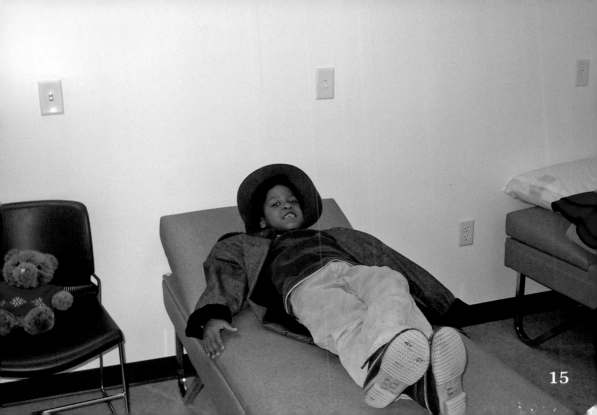

15

Dad is in the classroom.